Special thanks to Ryan Ferguson, Debra Mostow Zakarin, Kristine Lombardi,
Rita Lichtwardt, Nicole Corse, Karen Painter, Stuart Smith, Sammie Suchland,
Charnita Belcher, Julia Phelps, Julia Pistor, Renata Marchand, Michelle Cogan,
Kris Fogel, Arc Productions, Andrew Tan, Alexandra Kavalova, and Genna du Plessis

Published in the United States by Random House Children's Books,
a division of Penguin Random House LLC, 1745 Broadway, New York,
NY 10019, and in Canada by Penguin Random House Canada Limited,
Toronto.

Random House and the colophon are registered trademarks of
Penguin Random House LLC.

ISBN 978-1-101-94020-4 (trade) — ISBN 978-1-101-94021-1 (lib. bdg.) —
ISBN 978-1-101-94022-8 (ebook)
randomhousekids.com
Printed in the United States of America
10 9 8 7 6 5 4 3 2 1

Random House Children's Books supports the First Amendment and
celebrates the right to read.

Adapted by Mary Tillworth

**Based on the screenplay by
Kacey Arnold and Kate Boutilier**

**Illustrated by Charles Pickens and
Patrick Ian Moss**

Random House 🏠 New York

Deep in the forest, Barbie zoomed through the air. She rode a bright-pink hoverboard. She was so fast, she could fly with the Ava-Grun flock high above the trees!

Even though her home planet of Para-Den was just a tiny speck in the universe, Barbie loved it. There were no big cities or famous people. It was a beautiful planet where animals roamed freely. And at night, the stars gleamed like jewels.

As Barbie landed at home, a small creature with a pink tuft of fur flew to her.

Barbie hugged her pet. "Hi, Pupcorn!"

Barbie's father came outside. "I just got a message from King Constantine. He's asking for volunteers to travel to Opa-Irri for training. He needs them to reset the star fields. He wants your help."

Barbie was nervous. She had never been far from home. "Me? Why would the king want my help?"

"You made quite a name for yourself at the galactic playoffs last year. The king's scout must have seen how good you are on your hoverboard."

Barbie also had a special gift. If she focused hard, she could make things move. But she was still learning how to control

her powers. And resetting the star fields sounded like a huge task!

Later that night, Barbie sat on the porch. Her father joined her.

"What will happen if the stars don't reset?" Barbie asked.

Barbie's father looked sad. "They could disappear." He put an arm around his daughter. "The night you were born, the sky was alive with stars, swirling and spinning. It was like they were dancing just for you." He smiled. "That's why your mother called you her little Starlight."

Barbie gazed at the stars. Should she help the king? She searched her heart for the answer, like her mom had taught her. She knew what she had to do.

The next day, Barbie and her father flew to Opa-Irri, the planet where King Constantine lived.

Barbie's father landed at a huge spaceport. Barbie hopped out. "Wow!" She had never seen so many people!

Sleek buildings gleamed all around her. A statue of King Constantine towered over the city. A castle with silver walls and a tall gate loomed in the distance.

Barbie's father handed her a suitcase. "There are a few surprises in there."

Barbie unzipped the suitcase. Pupcorn jumped out! Underneath her furry pet, Barbie saw a shimmering dress.

"Your mother wanted you to have it." Barbie's father opened a bag. "And I have something else for you, too." He pulled out a new hoverboard.

"Dad, this is amazing!" Barbie hugged her father. "I love you."

Her father smiled. "Good luck, my little

Starlight. And remember—listen to your heart. It won't lead you wrong."

Barbie said goodbye to her father and put on her mother's dress. She headed to the royal castle.

When she reached the glittering throne room, she took a deep breath. "You can do this," she told herself.

"Quite a sight, isn't it?" said a voice behind her.

Barbie turned. A man with dark brown hair smiled at her. "I've never seen a king's castle up close," she admitted.

A party guest scurried over. "Prince Leo! Wonderful to see you."

Barbie gasped. "You're royalty?"

Prince Leo shrugged. "By birth. I'm Prince Leo of Kumai. But you can just call me plain Leo. I won't have you locked up in a crater."

Barbie laughed. Maybe royalty wasn't as scary as she had thought.

Meeting a royal like Prince Leo was easy. But King Constantine was a different story. He was a stern man who liked rules and had no sense of humor.

After the volunteers gathered in the ballroom, the king addressed them. "We have prepared a celebration for you." He frowned. "Enjoy it, but remember, your training starts tomorrow."

Barbie met the other volunteers. Prince Leo was the fastest pilot in the kingdom and a skilled engineer. Kareena and Sheena were telepathic twins who could move matter with their minds. And

Sal-lee was the intergalactic gold medalist for hoverboarding.

"You're the other hoverboarder?" Sal-lee asked Barbie.

"Well, yes, but I'm not as fast as you."

Barbie paused. "I've only won regionals."

The volunteers looked at her with interest. Then they were told to find their seats at the long dining table. Barbie and Leo walked over together but discovered that their seats were at opposite ends of the table.

Barbie hummed softly and switched the place cards with her mind. The twins squealed with excitement. They were thrilled to meet someone else who could move matter.

As they sat down, Barbie spotted a

familiar tuft of pink fur. "Pupcorn!"

"What is that?" asked Prince Leo.

"He's called a Pupcorn. But he hasn't popped yet." Barbie scooped Pupcorn onto her lap. "My dad says he could be anything."

Leo petted Pupcorn. "Hey, buddy. You could wind up like something in the king's zoo."

"The king has a zoo?" Barbie asked.

"The biggest in the galaxy. He fills it with exotic animals." Sal-lee wagged her finger. "So watch out—your Pupcorn could be next!"

Barbie held her pet close. "I'd like to see him try!"

Pupcorn squeaked in agreement.

After dinner, King Constantine opened the dance floor, but the music was slow. Barbie looked around. Everything about the party was so . . . orderly. The guests were yawning.

Barbie wanted to change things up. She focused on the energy in the room and tapped out a funky beat. The other volunteers joined in.

Soon the dance floor was rocking!

King Constantine stormed into the ballroom. "What is the meaning of this? This is not how we dance!"

"Isn't there more than one way to dance?" Barbie asked the king.

The king raised his hand. Slow music began to play again. King Constantine glared at Barbie. "In this castle, I make the rules."

Barbie wanted to sink into the floor. Working for the king was going to be harder than she had thought.

The next morning, the volunteers gathered in the training room. King Constantine introduced his assistant, a robot named Artemis. Artemis showed the volunteers a hologram of a distant planet.

"Our galaxy has fallen out of step with the universe," said Artemis. "According to the prophecy, if we do not get the stars to dance again, they will disappear."

Barbie couldn't imagine a world without stars.

"I have a plan," said the king. "I must gain access to the heart of the galaxy on

Central Planet. Since there are many obstacles in the way, I will need you all along for the journey."

He showed them a small machine. It had two feet that shuffled together. "This machine is called a Stato-tron. Its feet will make a high jolt of electricity that will reset the stars."

Barbie looked at the Stato-tron nervously. *Shocking the stars? That's not going to work,* she thought.

Leo had just leaned in to talk to Barbie when the king turned toward them. "Leo,

Barbie, thank you for volunteering for a warm-up match," he said.

Barbie and Prince Leo reappeared in another section of the holodeck. They had to use their agility and reflexes in a combat challenge. Barbie took Leo by surprise, knocking him down with a quick flip.

"That's enough! The fun and games are over!" shouted the king.

The training cubes rearranged to create a hoverboard track. Now Barbie and Sal-lee had to race around the track and use the twins' powers to get through the gravity fields. But when Barbie used her own matter-moving power to help Sal-lee, the king was intrigued.

King Constantine asked Barbie to break up a large training cube. He made the cube heavier and heavier until Barbie was too tired to keep trying.

That afternoon, Sal-lee visited Barbie. "The king was a little tough on you," she said.

"Huh? Oh, yeah, I guess so," Barbie said.

Sal-lee looked up at the stars. "About

what happened during the training . . . ,"
she began. "I wanted to say thank you."
Then, quickly changing the subject, Sal-lee
said, "Hey, your pet is growing whiskers!"
She smiled at Barbie and took off on her
hoverboard.

Barbie felt her heart lighten. It was
nice to have made a friend.

Pop!

Barbie looked down. A cat with wide
eyes and a pink tuft of hair looked up at
her.

"Pupcorn, you popped!" Barbie jumped

on her hoverboard. "Let's show everyone your transformation!"

Pupcorn meowed and tried to follow, but he had lost his ability to fly!

Barbie zipped around the castle, looking for the right materials. When she was done, she got to work. A little while later, Pupcorn was flying again—in his very own cat space suit!

King Constantine had one more challenge for the volunteers. "Your final test is to capture a Starlian."

"A Starlian?" cried Barbie. Starlians were gentle, peaceful creatures. "Why?"

"Just proceed!" barked the king.

The team flew to the Starlians' home planet. After searching for hours, they discovered a Starlian in a rocky forest.

Barbie looked at the animal. It had kind eyes. It reminded her of a creature on Para-Den that loved music.

Barbie drummed a soft beat. The other volunteers helped. Sal-lee tapped her hoverboard. The twins hummed a soothing tune. The Starlian stopped to listen.

"Now!" shouted Leo.

Kareena and Sheena blinded the Starlian with light. Sal-lee wrapped a rope around the creature. Leo threw a large net over it.

"We did it!" the team cheered.

Even though she should have felt
proud, Barbie was upset. The creature
looked so sad. "Why would the king want
a Starlian?" she asked.

Then she knew. Pupcorn had popped into an adorable cat. But if he had been something more exotic, the king might have put him in his zoo. And if the king could lock up Pupcorn, he could lock up a Starlian, too.

Barbie marched to the net. She cut the ropes. The Starlian raced off.

Barbie knew in her heart that she had done the right thing.

"You let the Starlian go?" King Constantine glared at Barbie from his throne. "Why?"

Barbie raised her chin. "A Starlian cannot survive in a zoo."

King Constantine shook his head. "I needed a Starlian to guide us to Central Planet. It is the only creature that can protect us from the magnetic storms."

Barbie gasped. "If you had just explained—"

"Explained? I am the king. I don't have to explain anything." King Constantine folded his arms. "Without a Starlian, who is going to get us safely to the center of the galaxy?"

Barbie hung her head. "I don't know."

The king scowled. "You are dismissed from this mission."

Barbie ran to her room. She was packing her bags when her father called on video chat. "I've ruined everything!" she cried.

"And now the mission could fail!"

"I'm sorry, hon," Barbie's father said. "I wish I knew how to fix this."

Barbie looked at her father. "That's it! I can't leave. I have to fix this."

Later that day, Sal-lee visited the king. "You need to bring Barbie back," she said. "I know she doesn't follow rules perfectly, but her instincts are right."

"Why are you defending her?" he asked. "You're a champion. She's not your equal."

Sal-lee nodded. "No. She's not." She

paused. "Barbie's better. She knows how to be a leader."

As Sal-lee finished, there was a roar outside the throne room. Barbie had returned—with a Starlian.

"He's here of his own free will," she announced.

King Constantine had no choice. "You are back on the team," he told Barbie.

King Constantine's spaceship set off for Central Planet. Barbie and her teammates watched the galaxy go by. They were finally going to reset the stars!

They passed through a magnetic storm. Fire and lightning flew toward them. The Starlian sprang into action. It protected the spaceship with its huge body.

As they neared the edge of the storm,

a chunk of boiling debris crashed into the ship!

"One of the thrusters has been damaged!" called Leo. He switched the ship to autopilot and put on a space suit. He crawled through the air lock and cleared the debris out of the thruster.

As Leo reached for the air lock to get back in, a rock knocked him off the ship!

"He's drifting away!" called Sal-lee.

Barbie acted fast. She told the twins to change the pull of the ship's gravity. As Leo was yanked toward the ship, Barbie

opened the air lock. Leo flew inside!

Everyone breathed a sigh of relief.

A few hours later, Central Planet came into view. The team landed on its dry and dusty surface.

"So, what's the plan?" asked Sal-lee.

King Constantine rolled out the Stato-tron. "Proceed."

Barbie and Sal-lee led the way. Soon they came to a glowing orb field. The orbs were sharp and prickly.

The twins changed the pull of gravity to move the orbs, clearing a path through the field. Barbie and Sal-lee rode on their hoverboards, followed by King Constantine and Leo.

The group passed the orb field and went into a tunnel. It was quiet and peaceful as they came across a huge cavern with an open ceiling. Stars shone down on them. They had found the altar of the stars!

"**W**hoa. It's stunning!" Barbie breathed.

"Never mind that." King Constantine dragged the Stato-tron deeper into the cavern. After a while, he called, "We're here—the heart of the galaxy."

It was a stunning replica of the galaxy. One bright star floated in the middle. It pulsed steadily.

The king wrapped the Stato-tron around the heart of the galaxy. He flipped a switch.

The Stato-tron rubbed its feet. It created a huge jolt of electricity. But instead of being powered up, the stars began to fade.

Barbie remembered her father's words: *Listen to your heart. It won't lead you wrong.*

The stars continued to go dark, and some even fell. Barbie caught a single star. She knew what to do. She closed her eyes and tuned in to the beats around her.

The star in her hand began to shine brightly. Barbie sang and scooped up a handful of stars. They glimmered to life.

Barbie began to glow like the stars. As she sang, the stars glowed and danced

around her. They turned her space suit into a shimmering gown.

Leo, Sal-lee, and the twins sang with her. The more they sang, the brighter the stars became. Stars twinkled and twirled.

They exploded out of the tunnel in a rush of light. Barbie and her friends had reset the stars!

"You did it," King Constantine said in awe.

"We just needed to look up and dance," said Barbie.

The team stood in a circle and joined hands, staring at the stars shining brightly above them.

They went back to the spaceship. The Starlian was still there. And he had invited his friends.

Barbie and the others boarded the spaceship. Protected by the Starlians, they flew back to Opa-Irri. All around them, the stars danced and spun.

Back at the castle, King Constantine threw the volunteers a party. And because Barbie had made the stars shine again, he crowned her the Starlight Princess!

During the celebration, the king pulled Barbie aside. "I was wrong about you. You're not disruptive or threatening. You think for yourself. You're full of life—just like the galaxy you saved."

"*Helped* save," Barbie corrected him.

King Constantine smiled. "I was thinking maybe you could stay on Opa-Irri and help me run things."

Barbie gasped. "I don't know if I'm ready for that yet. I question things. I still act before I think—"

The king held up his hand. "I could learn from you. And perhaps you could learn from me." He gestured to the rest of the volunteers. "You must admit, I did assemble a good team."

Barbie thought about it. "Maybe I could